Bindiya in India

Written by
Monique Kamaria Chheda, MD

Illustrated by
Debasmita Dasgupta

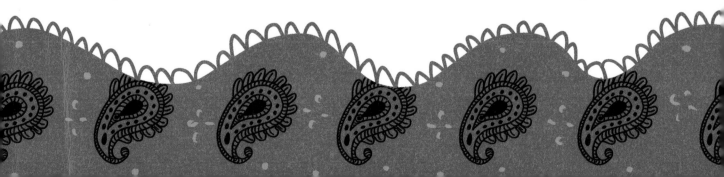

Stepping off the plane
she looks all around.

and sees her family
waiting on the ground.

They say "hi beta"
and give a hug.
Then her cousins
give her hand a tug.

She watches the couple share sweet *prasad*, as they sit in *puja* and pray to God.

yummy

प्रसाद

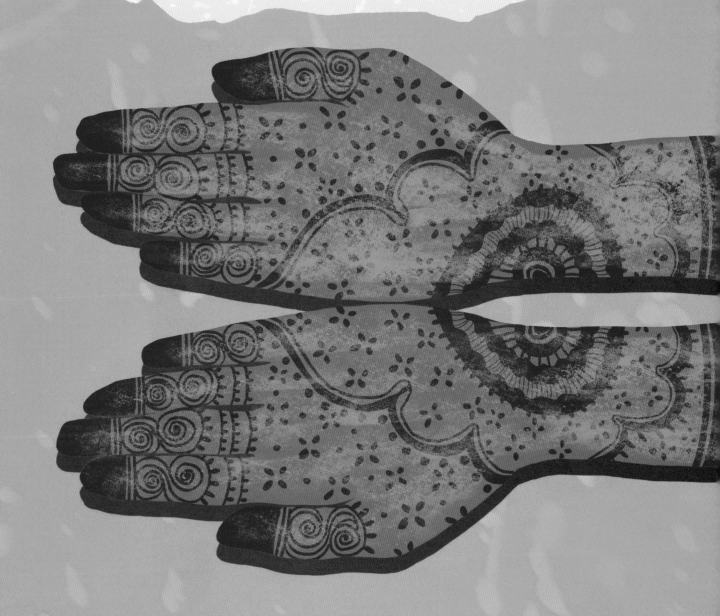

Watching it turn red
the longer it stands

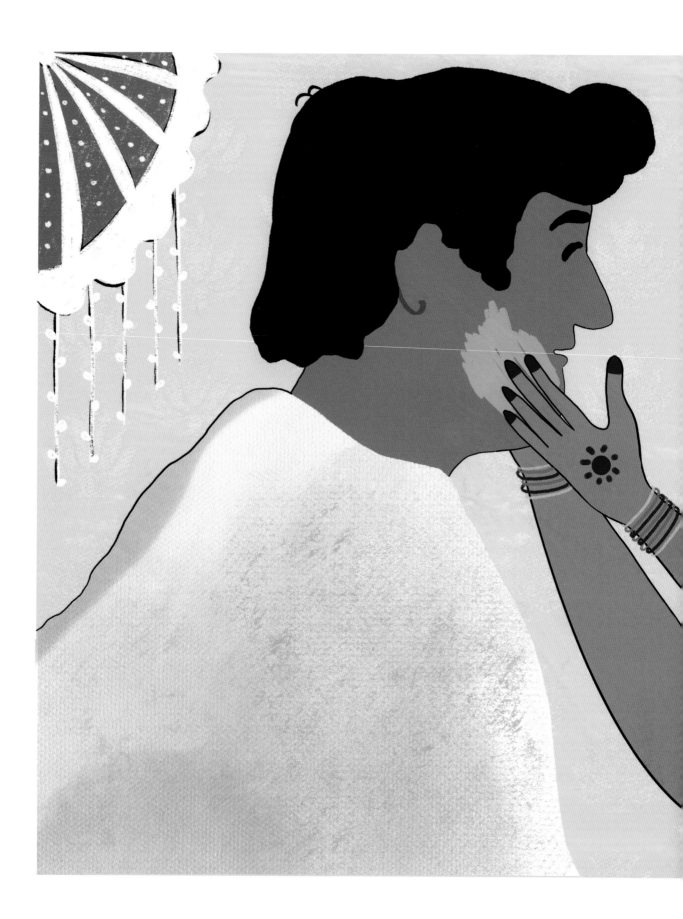

Spreading **haldi** paste on the groom, laughter and joy fill the whole room.

हल्दी time

Eating and greeting
at the sangeet.

She follows the Dulha
on a haathi.

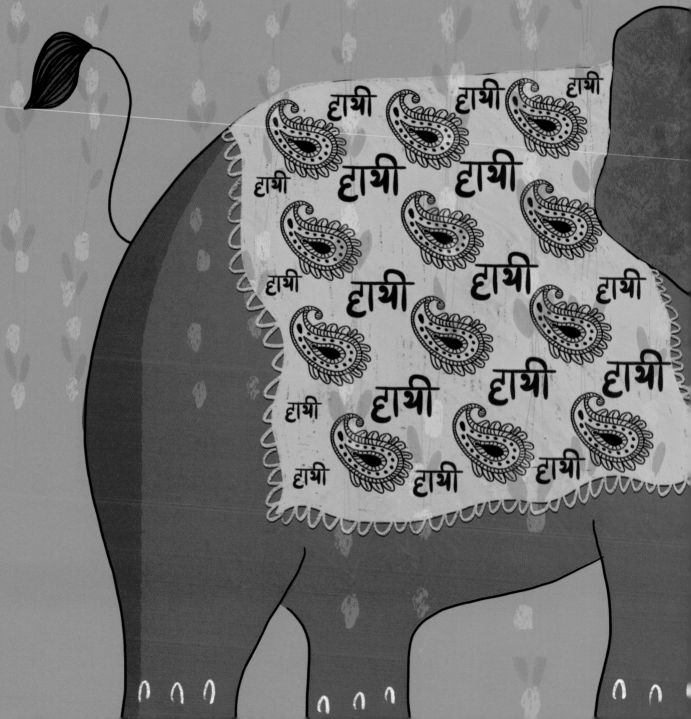

happily going to wed
his *saathi.*

She spies a *bandar* jumping on a roof, and a dog roaming freely, barking "woof."

Spotting the mandap
so beautiful and bold.

She sees the bride
adorned with gold.

As the couple walks
around the fire,
she watches
the wedding rituals transpire.

beautiful
मंडप

Celebrating with family
on her final night,
she thinks aloud,
"what an amazing sight."

Looking up
at the stars and moon,
she smiles,
knowing she will be
back soon.

Glossary & Pronunciation Guide

Beta (beh-Ta) — Child

Shaadi (shaa-DEE) — Wedding

Gaadi (gaa-DEE) — Car

Nana (na-NA) — Grandfather- mother' s father

Nani (na-NEE) — Grandmother- mother's mother

Kahaani (kuh-ha-NEE) — Story/tale

Prasad (pruh-sahd) — Religious blessing in the form of food

Pooja (POO-jah) — Prayer

Mehndi (mehn-DHEE) — Henna

Haldi (hul-DHEE) — Turmeric

Sangeet (sun-GEET) — Musical night before the wedding

Dulha (DOOL-ha) — Groom

Haathi (ha-THEE) — Elephant

Saathi (sa-THEE) — Partner

Baraat (ba-RAAT) — Groom's wedding procession

Geet (geet) — Song

Bandar (BUN-dhur) — Monkey

Mandap (MUN-dup) — Altar

Parivaar (pur-ee-VAR) — Family

Monique Chheda, MD (Author): Monique Chheda is a dermatologist living in Maryland. She is married and has two young children. Becoming a mother inspired her to revive one of her hobbies, writing. Wanting to pass on her Indian culture to her children, she found a scarcity of children's books that allowed Indian-American children to connect with their heritage. This prompted her to write her own children's book, *Bindiya in India.* Her hope is that through literature, she can share India's rich culture and language with the next generation.

Debasmita Dasgupta (Illustrator): Debasmita Dasgupta is a Kirkus-Best Prize-nominated internationally-published picture-book illustrator and graphic novelist based in Singapore. With a decade of experience in the field of art-for-change, she works with mixed media, marrying ink, paint, and digital tools to create diverse fiction and non-fiction visual stories for children and young adults. She has illustrated over twenty picture books, comics, and poems, and her art has been exhibited across the globe.